LBC MIDDLE SCHOOL
LIBRARY

OAKLAND

RICHARD RAMBECK

THE HISTORY OF THE
ATHLETICS

CREATIVE EDUCATION

Published by Creative Education
123 South Broad Street, Mankato, Minnesota 56001
Creative Education is an imprint of The Creative Company

Designed by Rita Marshall
Editorial assistance by Neil Bernards & John Nichols

Photos by: Allsport Photography, Focus on Sports, SportsChrome.

Copyright © 1999 Creative Education.
International copyrights reserved in all countries.
No part of this book may be reproduced in any form without written permission from the publisher.
Printed in the United States of America.

Library of Congress Cataloging-in-Publication Data

Rambeck, Richard.
The History of the Oakland A's / by Richard Rambeck.
p. cm. — (Baseball)
Summary: A team history of the "A's," born in Philadelphia, once resided in Kansas City, and now settled in Oakland, where for more than 20 years they have been highly successful.
ISBN: 0-88682-919-4

1. Oakland Athletics (Baseball team)—History—Juvenile literature.
[1. Oakland Athletics (Baseball team)—History. 2. Baseball—History.]
I. Title. II. Series: Baseball (Mankato, Minn.)

GV875.O24R36   1999
796.357'64'0979466—dc21   97-9231

First edition

9 8 7 6 5 4 3 2 1

The East Bay hills tower over Oakland, rising from the water's edge to a wooded crest hundreds of feet above the port city. Standing atop the hills, you can view the entire Bay Area, from Berkeley and the Golden Gate Bridge on the north, to San Francisco and Navy Island on the west. The rolling hills seem to cradle the city, looking down on landmarks like the stately Bay Bridge and Oakland's Alameda County stadium.

Called the Jewel of the East Bay, Oakland was founded in 1854 in response to the great California gold rush. By 1900, it had grown to a city of 60,000 whose workers provided the

All-time Athletics great "Home Run" Baker.

Hall-of-Famer Nap LaJoie hit .422 and won the American League's first Triple Crown.

labor to make the area prosper. They unloaded cargo ships, loaded trains, and built bridges across the bay to their glamorous sister city: San Francisco. While San Francisco became an international city of fame, beauty, and wealth, Oakland quietly worked in its shadow.

Today, with a population of 372,000, Oakland supports three professional sports teams: basketball's Golden State Warriors, football's Raiders, and baseball's Athletics. Oakland fans are extremely loyal to their teams, and sports is one area where Oakland does not take a back seat to San Francisco. In fact, the Athletics, or "A's" as they are more commonly known, have been one of baseball's most successful teams over the last three decades.

Since 1971, The A's have won 10 American League West Division titles, six league pennants, and four World Series championships. No other major-league team has claimed as many division titles or World Series victories in as short a time span. The story of the Athletics' franchise is one of success and one of failure. It is also a tale of three cities: Philadelphia, Kansas City, and Oakland.

LONG ROAD TO OAKLAND

The Athletics were born in 1901 nearly 3,000 miles from Oakland, in Philadelphia. The driving force behind that first team was baseball legend Cornelius McGillicuddy, or Connie Mack, who owned and managed the team for an amazing 50 years. Mack's place in baseball history was established as he led the Athletics to nine American League pennants and five World Series titles during his tenure.

Future star, outfielder Ben Grieve.

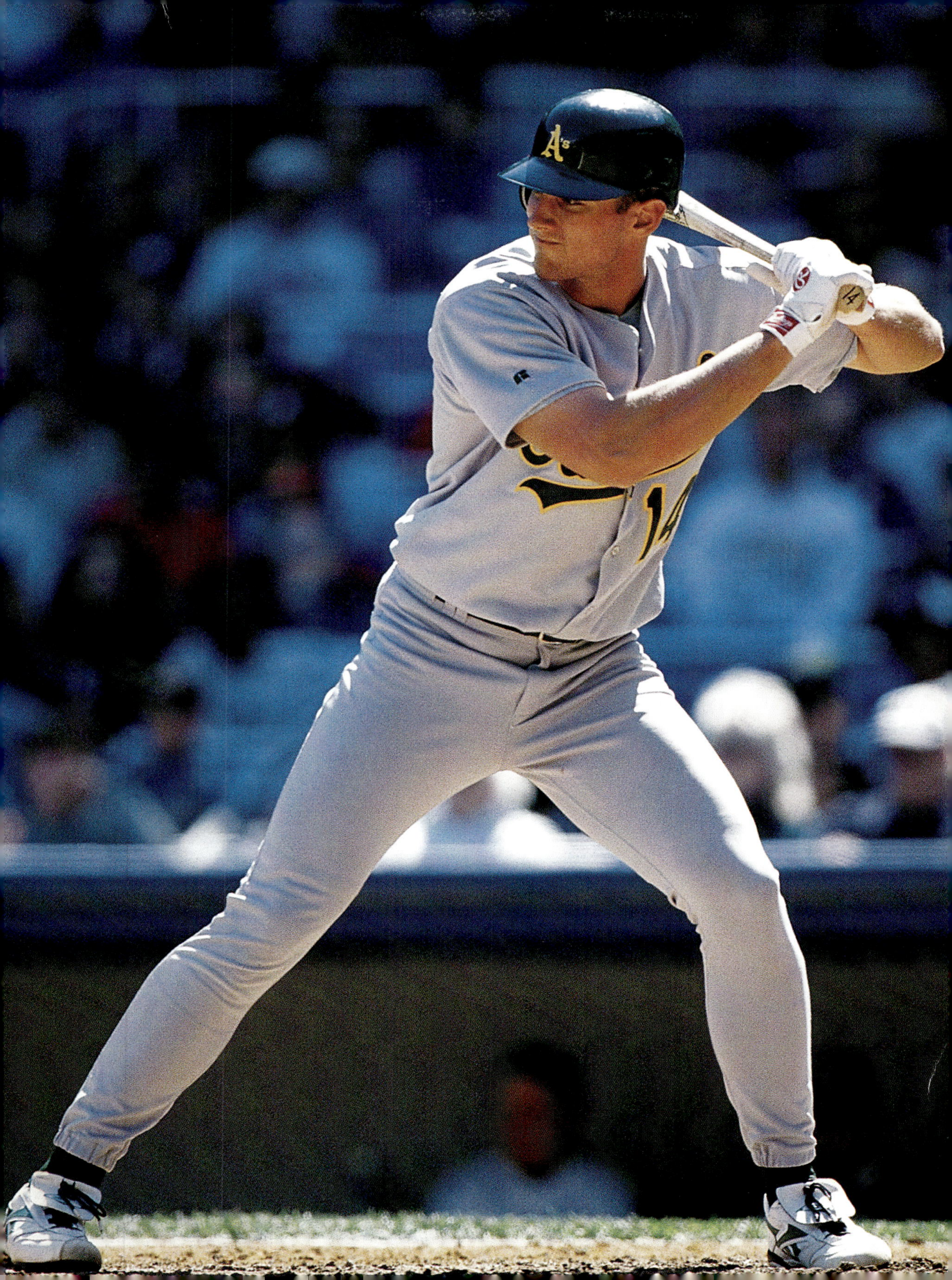
14

1929

Howard Ehmke set a World Series record by striking out 13 batters in the opening victory over Chicago.

Philadelphia dominated the American League from 1910 to 1914, winning four pennants in five years. The team was built around the fabulous talents of a pair of hard-hitting infielders: third baseman Eddie Collins and second baseman Frank "Home Run" Baker. Unfortunately, Mack's baseball genius was only exceeded by his tight-fisted ways with money. Over the years, he would consistently build his teams into contenders, only to sell his stars off when they became too expensive.

Mack's financial problems began in earnest when a new baseball league—the short-lived Federal League—was formed in 1913. Federal League owners paid higher salaries to lure players from American and National League teams. It was like modern-day free agency. Most American League and National League teams kept their stars by matching the offers of Federal League clubs, but not Mack. He refused to be pushed around by other baseball owners. Consequently, the Athletics lost star pitchers Charles Albert "Chief" Bender and Eddie Plank to the new league and, as a result, a talent shortage hurt the club for more than 10 years.

Mack managed to rebuild the team by the mid-1920s. At the end of that decade, Philadelphia once again rose to the top of the American League. The Athletics featured a collection of great hitters, including Al Simmons, catcher Mickey Cochrane, Bing Miller, and the unbelievably strong Jimmy Foxx. "Foxx has muscles in his hair," joked teammate Bob Johnson. After giving up a particularly long home run to the muscular A's first baseman, Yankees pitcher Lefty Gomez quipped, "Foxx wasn't scouted, he was trapped." Foxx, nicknamed "The Beast" by his teammates, hit 58 homers in 1932, a figure that still stands as the third-highest season total ever.

Along with their powerful offense, the A's also had quality pitching. Lefty Grove, George Earnshaw, and George "Rube" Walberg gave Philadelphia a starting rotation matched by few teams. These stars rocketed the Athletics to three-straight American League pennants from 1929 to 1931 and World Series titles in 1929 and 1930. After winning the 1931 pennant, though, the team was never able to recapture its glory days. Mack again was unable to pay his stars, and one by one, they were sold off to other teams. In fact, the team's record became so consistently bad that fans stopped coming to games. In 1955, the A's picked up and headed west to Kansas City, Missouri.

Despite a new city, excited fans, and an expanding baseball league, the Kansas City Athletics did not fare well. In its 13 years in Kansas City, the team never finished higher than sixth. Its owner finally gave up and sold out to a brash young businessman named Charles O. Finley in December 1960. Finley paid $3.8 million for the club (a bargain by today's standards).

Finley, often called Charlie O, was a wealthy man with big ideas. He was creative, stubborn, and confident. Although his personality often wore thin with his managers, coaches, and players, he eventually built the A's into the best team in baseball. In fact, the Athletics became only the second franchise in major-league history—the other being the New York Yankees—to win World Series championships three years in a row.

The A's moved to Kansas City and finished sixth in the league under manager Lou Boudreau.

Athletics slugger, Dave Henderson.

The magical Dennis Eckersley.

"CATFISH" AND REGGIE SPARK A'S UPRISING

1 9 6 8

All-Star shortstop Bert Campaneris led the Oakland club in hits, runs, at-bats, and triples.

Charles Finley's success with the Oakland A's actually began in Kansas City. In 1962, he signed shortstop Bert Campaneris as a free agent. Two years later, pitcher Jim Hunter joined the team. After signing Hunter, Finley decided that the pitcher needed a nickname to spark fan interest. He asked Hunter where he was from. Hunter told the owner he grew up on a farm in North Carolina. Finley immediately dreamed up a story about how Hunter had gotten in trouble as a youth for going fishing instead of doing his chores. "Just tell the press when they ask about it that your dad couldn't bring himself to punish you because of the big stringer of catfish you had caught," said Finley. "And that's how you got the name 'Catfish' Hunter."

Finley's endless scheming and his opinionated nature tended to overshadow the fact that he knew baseball talent. Along with Hunter, Finley brought stars such as catcher Gene Tenace, outfielder Joe Rudi, and relief pitcher Rollie Fingers to the A's. In 1965, Finley drafted and signed standout third baseman and team leader Sal Bando. Slugging outfielder Reggie Jackson was selected in the 1966 draft, and hard-throwing pitcher Vida Blue was drafted a year later.

By 1967, the team was starting to improve, but not enough to keep Kansas City fans interested. Due to lack of fan support, the A's again moved west in 1968. This time they chose Oakland. That year, Hunter threw the first regular-season perfect game by an American League pitcher in 46 years. Against the hard-hitting Minnesota Twins, Hunter allowed no hits, no walks, and no base runners: a perfect game.

Besides his pitching leadership, Hunter was a calm, cool presence in the locker room, a constant inspiration to his teammates. Led by Hunter's heroics, the 1969 Oakland A's compiled a winning record of 88–74 to finish second in the AL West Division. (In 1969 the American League expanded from 10 to 12 teams and was divided into two divisions, East and West.)

The improving A's were a big story in 1969, but the hitting of Reggie Jackson was an even bigger sensation. For much of the season, Jackson hit home runs so often that many fans thought he would break Roger Maris's single-season record of 61 homers. The pressure on the 23-year-old slugger became incredible; he was the biggest fan attraction in the majors. Jackson cooled off, however, and finished the year with 47 homers, second in the league behind Minnesota's Harmon Killebrew.

Jackson became one of the best home-run hitters in the American League. "When you hit a terrific shot," Jackson said, "all the players come to rest at that moment and watch you. Everyone is helpless and in awe. You charge people up by hitting the long ball."

Jackson, however, fell into an awful slump in 1970, when he batted just .237 with 23 home runs and 66 RBIs. "I'm trying, really trying," Jackson explained to the press during the season. "Maybe too hard. But the slump has made me a better person."

Jackson and the A's wound up second in the AL West in 1970—a good finish, but not good enough for demanding owner Charlie Finley. He fired manager John McNamara and replaced him with Dick Williams, who had led the Boston Red

Oakland third baseman Sal Bando set a club record by earning 118 walks.

Sox from nowhere in 1966 to the top of the American League in 1967. Williams knew what it took to win championships, something the Athletics' franchise had not done in 40 years.

A'S BEGIN WORLD SERIES RUN

In 1971, everything finally fell into place for the club. Young pitcher Vida Blue put together a dream season of 24 victories, a 1.82 earned-run average, and 301 strikeouts, all of which topped the American League. For his efforts, Blue was named the American League Cy Young Award winner, as well as the AL Most Valuable Player. Blue and other Oakland pitchers got plenty of support from Don Mincher (32 home runs), Sal Bando (24 home runs), and first baseman Mike Epstein (19 home runs).

Oakland won the AL West with an amazing 101–60 record, but the team's luck ran out in the league championship series. Oakland lost to the Baltimore Orioles in the best-of-five series, allowing the Orioles to advance to their third-straight World Series. The A's had put together the franchise's best year since 1931, but the team went home disappointed. Still, the young A's were eager for the next season to begin.

In 1972, Oakland roared to its second-straight AL West title and defeated the Detroit Tigers in the league championship series. For the first time in 41 years, the A's were in the World Series. Baseball experts gave the team little chance to defeat Cincinnati and the stars of the "Big Red Machine"—Johnny Bench, Joe Morgan, and Pete Rose—especially since Reggie Jackson was injured and could not play.

But the A's shocked the baseball world by winning the

1 9 7 2

The A's colorful owner, Charlie Finley, was named The Sporting News *Sportsman of the Year.*

A's slugger Reggie Jackson.

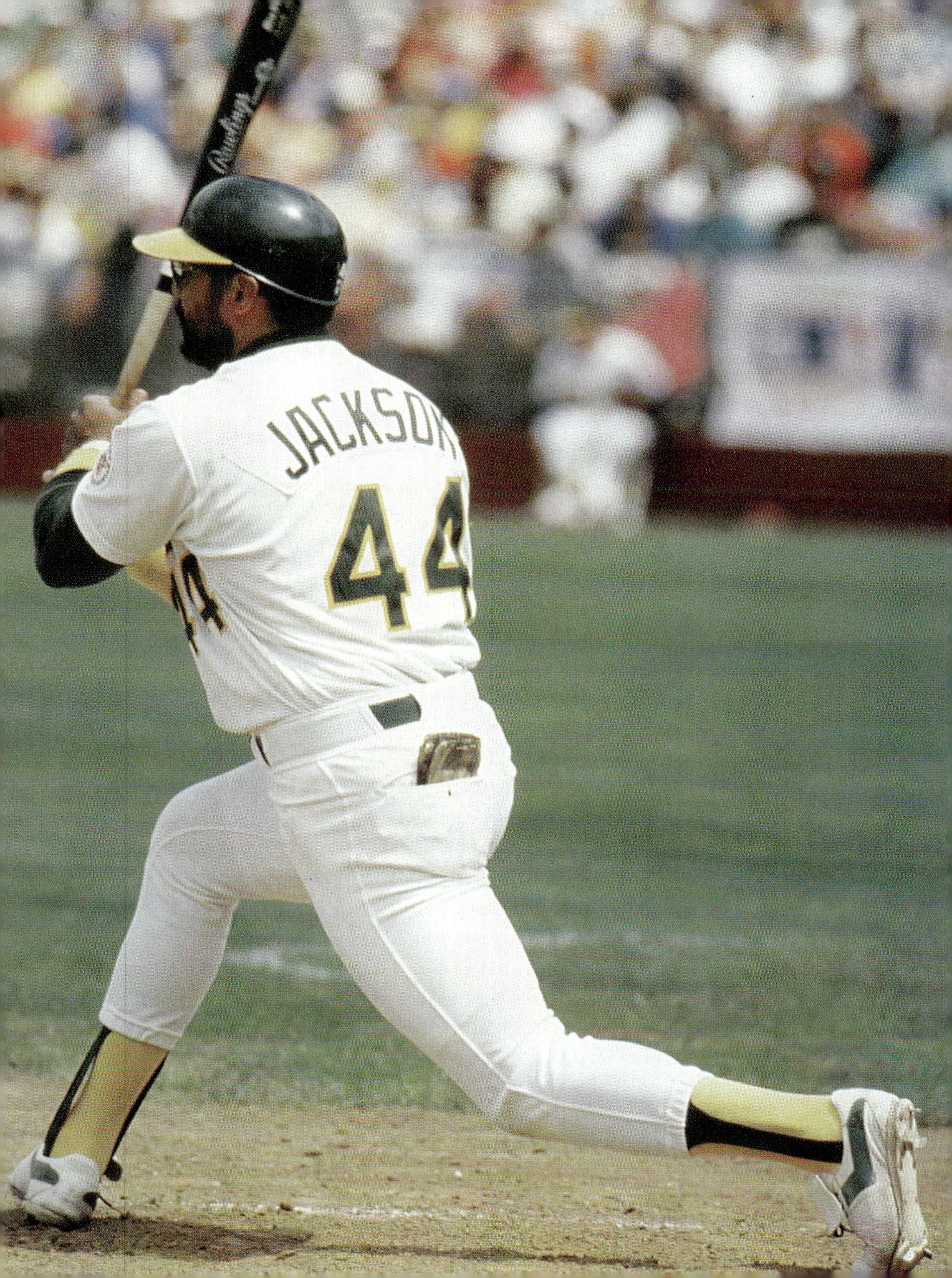
JACKSON
44

An Oakland star of the late 1980s, Dave Stewart.

series four games to three. Catcher Gene Tenace, who had gotten only one hit in 17 at bats against Detroit in the American League Championship Series, was a big reason for the upset. In the World Series, Tenace knocked out four home runs, drove in nine RBIs, and batted .348 to win the Most Valuable Player award.

After winning the 1972 World Series, the A's coasted to the 1973 AL West title behind Jackson, who led the American League in RBIs (117), and also contributed 32 home runs. For his efforts, Jackson was named the league's Most Valuable Player. Oakland then defeated Baltimore to advance to the World Series for the second-straight year. For Jackson, playing in the World Series was something new since he had missed the 1972 series. He vowed to make the most of his chance in 1973. Jackson came through and began a long history of performing at his best in the World Series, a habit that would later earn him the nickname "Mr. October." Behind his hitting, the A's defeated the New York Mets four games to three, and Jackson was named MVP.

Despite the team's success, Dick Williams stepped down as manager. He grew tired of Finley's demanding ways and unpredictable outbursts. Finley replaced Williams with Alvin Dark, who had managed the A's once before in Kansas City. Under Dark, the powerful A's rolled to their fourth-straight division title and third-consecutive American League pennant, beating the Baltimore Orioles again in the league championship series.

In the 1974 regular season, it was "Catfish" Hunter's turn to be the Athletics' hero. During the season, Hunter posted 25 victories, the most in the American League, and was

Talented Oakland outfielder Joe Rudi won his second Gold Glove award in three years.

Oakland slugger Jose Canseco (pages 18-19).

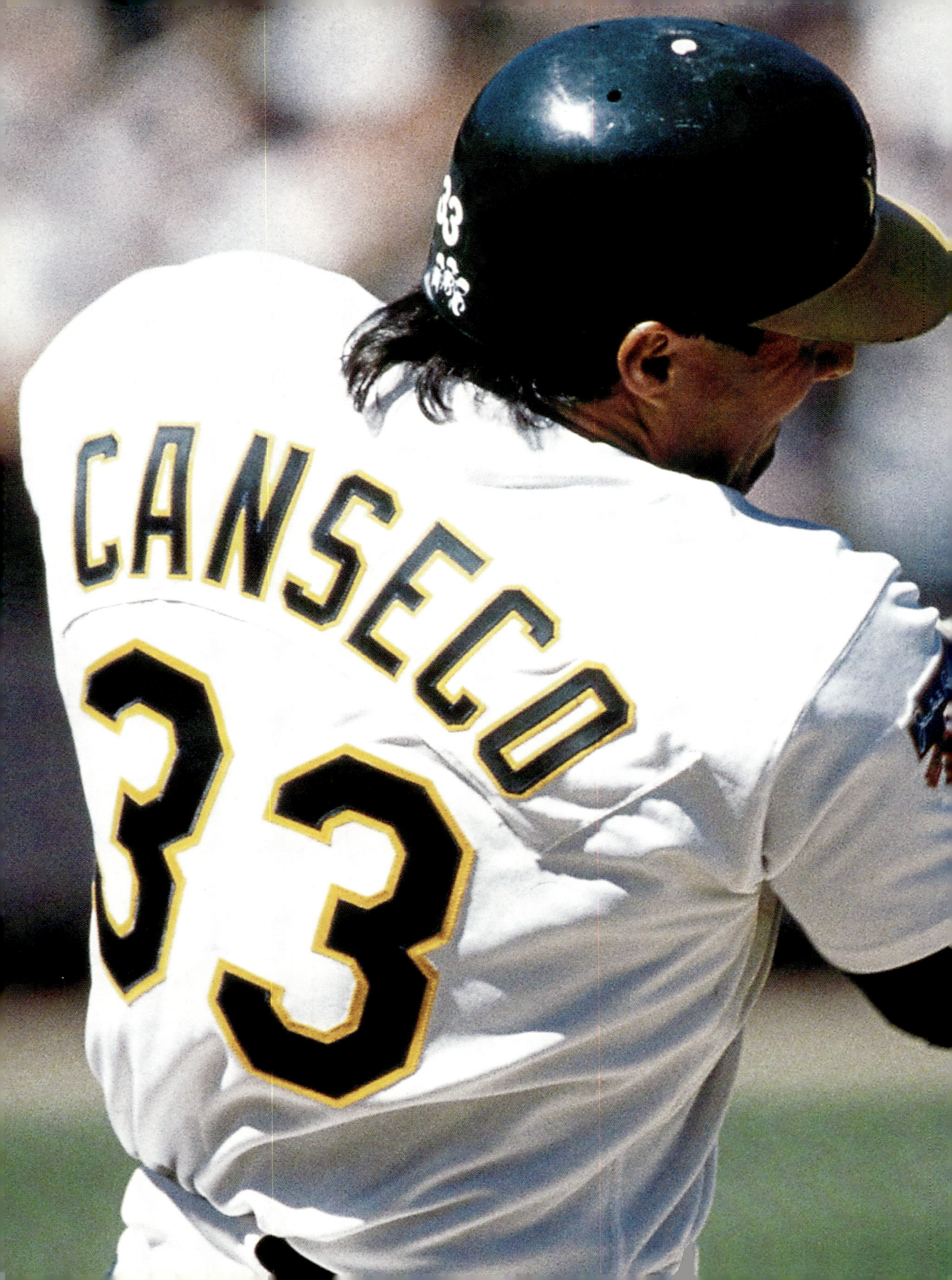
CANSECO
33

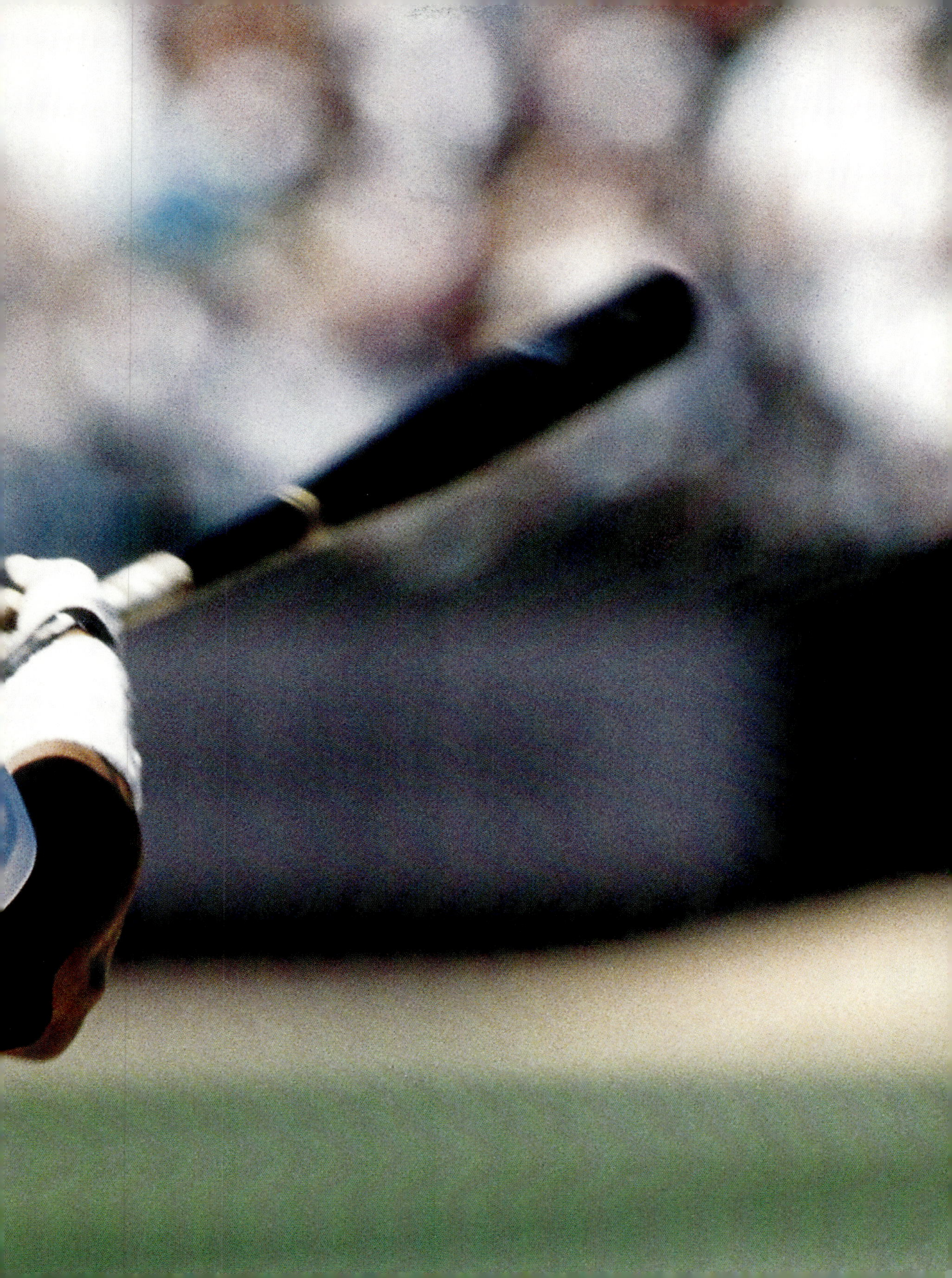

Outfielder Tony Armas belted 22 homers to lead the league during the strike-shortened playing season.

honored with the Cy Young Award. In the World Series, however, another Oakland pitcher stood at center stage. Reliever Rollie Fingers nailed down two saves and was named the Most Valuable Player as Oakland defeated the Los Angeles Dodgers four games to one.

The victory over the Dodgers made the A's only the second team in major-league history to win three straight World Series titles. Oakland fans had high hopes the team's success would continue. It did not.

The A's suffered a major blow before the 1975 season began. Hunter signed with the New York Yankees as a free agent, leaving the A's staff short-handed. Oakland still managed to win its fifth straight division title in 1975, but without Hunter, they lost to the Boston Red Sox in the league championship, three games to zero. Soon afterward, the financially strapped Finley—like Connie Mack before him—was forced to sell off the remaining pieces of his dynasty because he couldn't afford them.

The most bitter pill for Oakland fans to swallow was Finley's trade of Jackson to the Baltimore Orioles. The A's quickly fell from the top of the American League West to the bottom. Oakland fans soon lost interest in the team, and Finley faded from the spotlight. He sold the last-place A's to a group led by Walter A. Haas Jr. in 1979. After this, changes came quickly. The first was to name the infamous Billy Martin as the team's manager.

BILLY-BALL GETS A'S BACK INTO SWING

Under Billy Martin's direction, the A's of 1980 were transformed from a doormat to a contender. Outfielder Tony Armas slammed 35 homers and drove in 109 runs. Another young outfielder, Rickey Henderson, also blossomed, stealing an American League-record 100 bases. In addition, Oakland's starting pitchers completed 94 of 162 games, an astounding number in the modern era where relief pitchers are used frequently. "I figure the ball ain't heavy, and our starters tired are a lot better than our relievers rested, so I let them finish," explained Martin.

The new-look A's recaptured the hearts of their fans. Thousands came to Oakland's Alameda County Coliseum to watch what everyone called Billy-Ball in honor of the fiery Martin's leadership. After posting a second-place 83–79 record in 1980, the A's stormed from the gate in 1981 and won the AL West title in a season shortened by a players' strike. After defeating the Kansas City Royals in the first round of the playoffs, Martin lead his young A's into the league championship series against the team he had previously played for and managed, the New York Yankees. Coincidentally, Martin's A's would face a Yankees team lead by former Athletics' slugger Reggie Jackson. Jackson and the Yankees would win the matchup three games to none.

In 1982, Oakland starting pitchers Mike Norris, Rick Langford, and Steve McCatty all developed arm trouble. Many experts believed that the two years of Martin's hard-driving innings were to blame for their injuries. With no pitching to support them, and despite a tremendous season from

For the third consecutive year, Athletics outfielder Rickey Henderson was named to the AL All-Star team.

1 9 8 6

Mark McGwire hit his first major league homer off Walt Terrell at Detroit on August 25.

Henderson, who set the major-league record for steals in one season with 130, the ailing A's stumbled to a 68–94 record. The always volatile Martin had worn out his welcome in Oakland, and at season's end he resigned. "Billy gave the organization its pride back," said Henderson. "But the losing this year ate him up. He couldn't handle it."

By the mid-1980s, the A's were still struggling to regain their championship form. Steve Boros and Jackie Moore were both hired and fired as Oakland managers. After Moore was canned in the middle of the 1986 season, the A's hired Tony La Russa, who had led the Chicago White Sox to the American League West Division title in 1983. La Russa inherited a team that was long on ability but short on confidence. Working to instill the missing piece, the new manager put

A's shortstop Alfredo Griffin.

his faith in particular players to become leaders. One such player was pitcher Dave Stewart.

STEWART MAKES HIS PITCH FOR GREATNESS

In the first game Tony La Russa managed with the A's, Dave Stewart, a pitcher more known for his temper than his talent, got the victory. For the rest of the 1986 season, Stewart was the hottest pitcher in the American League, posting a 9–1 record. The secret to Stewart's success was a new pitch he had learned from pitching coach Dave Duncan—a forkball, a pitch that approaches the plate like a fastball, then suddenly sinks as the batter swings. Baseball experts were convinced that even with his new weapon, Stewart, who had failed with both the Los Angeles Dodgers and Texas Rangers beforehand, would return to his old self-destructive ways in 1987. But he did not. In fact, he won 20 games, the first of four straight 20-win seasons for Stewart. "Dave uses the same energy that used to hurt him—anger—to now help him concentrate and focus," said Duncan. "Where before he was all over the place emotionally, now he's all business."

Despite the efforts of Stewart and a record-shattering 49 home-run performance by Rookie of the Year first baseman Mark McGwire (most home runs in a season by a first-year player), the A's came up just short in the AL West race in 1987, losing out to the eventual World Series champion Minnesota Twins. But in 1988, there was no stopping Oakland and powerful right fielder Jose Canseco. Canseco, who was voted the 1986 American League Rookie of the Year, just kept getting better. He led the league in homers (42) and the

In his first season as Oakland manager, Tony LaRussa predicted a world championship "in five years or less."

team in steals (40), thus becoming the inaugural major-league player in the 40–40 club. The muscular, Cuban-born slugger was named the American League Most Valuable Player for his accomplishment.

Many thought Canseco's talent was just a natural gift, but those around him knew how much effort went into making him great. Canseco's manager also praised the power hitter's work habits. "I don't think the average person has any idea of the amount of effort that goes into the kind of play he's giving us," La Russa said. "And I don't mean just hitting. I'm looking at the whole package—his defense, his base-running. He plays this game intelligently."

Led by Canseco, the A's had a great 1988 season. They won 104 games to claim the AL West Division title and then swept the Boston Red Sox four games to none in the American League Championship Series. The Athletics were heavily favored to beat the Los Angeles Dodgers in the World Series. However, Oakland star relief pitcher Dennis Eckersley gave up a dramatic ninth-inning homer to the Dodgers' Kirk Gibson in the first game that gave Los Angeles a 5–4 victory. The A's never recovered from that blow, and the Dodgers won the series four games to one.

Walt Weiss was named AL Rookie of the Year in recognition of his fine overall play.

A'S FINALLY REACH THE TOP

After their disappointment in the 1988 series, the A's rebounded to win another division title in 1989, despite the fact that outfielder Jose Canseco missed almost half the season with an injury. Dave Stewart continued his dominance of AL hitters, and Mark McGwire, outfielder Dave

Henderson, and designated hitter Dave Parker made up for any power shortage caused by Canseco's absence. Oakland defeated Toronto four games to one in the league championship series and advanced to play cross-bay rival San Francisco in the World Series.

In the series, Stewart and Mike Moore held the power-hitting Giants to only one run in the first two games, pitching the A's to easy victories. Then the series shifted to San Francisco's Candlestick Park for game three. Just prior to game time, the entire Bay Area was rocked by a devastating earthquake. The series was postponed,to be resumed more than a week later. The delay did not harm Oakland at all. The A's won games three and four, sweeping the series four games to none. Stewart, who won twice in the series, was named the Most Valuable Player.

Slugging first baseman Mark McGwire was selected for his sixth consecutive All-Star Game.

The A's nearly duplicated their 1989 success the following season. Pitcher Bob Welch won an amazing 27 games, the most victories by any major-league pitcher in 22 years. In addition, Stewart won 22 games, and the A's claimed another division title and posted a record of 103–59, the best win-loss mark in baseball. Most experts picked Oakland to roll to another World Series title.

After sweeping the Boston Red Sox four games to none in the American League Championship Series, Oakland expected to defeat the Cincinnati Reds in the World Series. The Reds, however, used strong pitching and timely hitting to take four straight games from the surprised A's. Oakland and its fans had to settle for second-best for the second time in three years. "It seems we're a little snake-bit when we get to the series," observed Stewart. "We're always the favorites, so

New Bay Area basher Matt Stairs (pages 26-27).

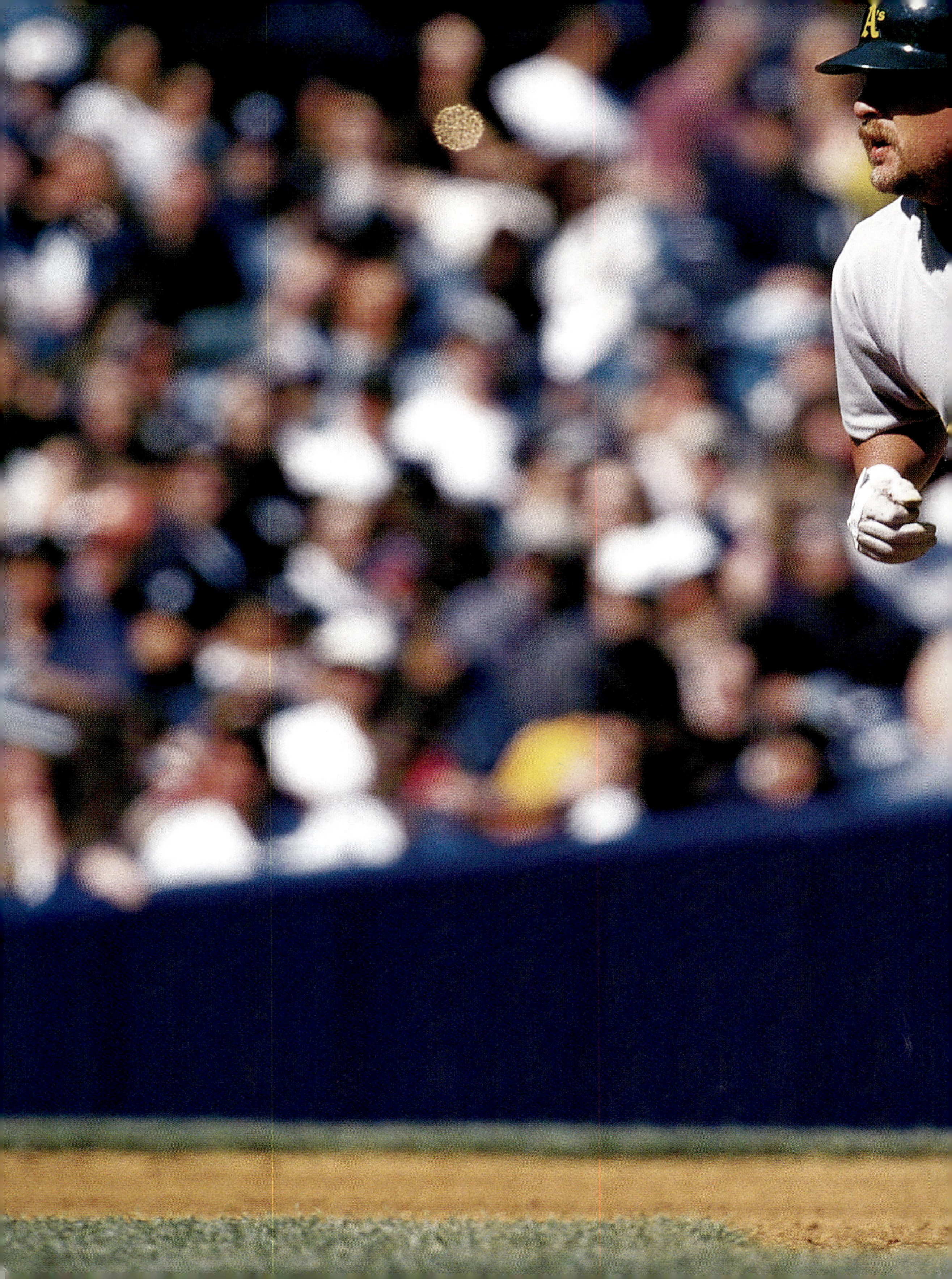

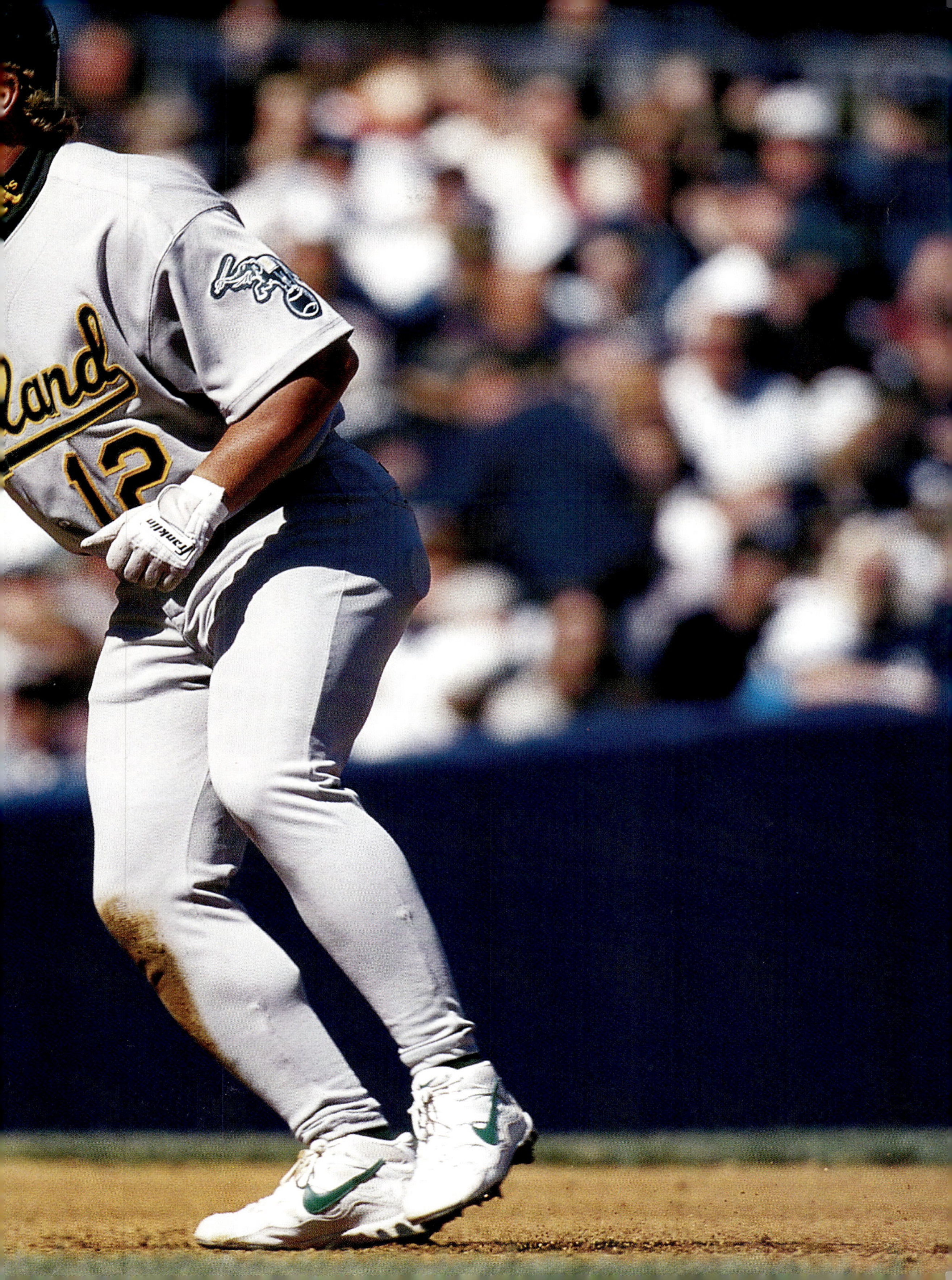

land
12

everybody comes gunning hard for us. No excuses, though; we just got whipped."

After a fourth-place division finish in 1991, the A's stormed back to win the American League West by six games in 1992. Behind the leadership of first baseman McGwire, the pitching of Dave Stewart, and the base-stealing of Rickey Henderson, the team rolled to a record of 96–66. However, the A's bid for postseason glory ended prematurely at the hands of the Toronto Blue Jays, who captured the league championship series four games to two. "It's sad that we couldn't win it this year, because you only get so many chances," noted a disappointed Stewart. "We've had a few, but you never know if it's going to be your last."

Second baseman Brent Gates set a team record by getting a hit in eight consecutive at-bats on May 23–24.

CHANGES COME TO OAKLAND

As the 1992 season ended in disappointment, the A's shocked the baseball world by trading star outfielder Jose Canseco to the Texas Rangers for outfielder Ruben Sierra and pitchers Jeff Russell and Bobby Witt. In addition, they later traded talented shortstop Walt Weiss to the expansion Florida Marlins. Also, All-Star pitcher Dave Stewart was allowed to sign with the Blue Jays and Mike Moore with the Detroit Tigers. Clearly, the Athletics' management had an eye on rebuilding the team with young talent. Even Rickey Henderson, major league baseball's leading career base stealer, was allowed to leave, and in 1996 closer Dennis Eckersley, the last link to the great A's teams of the late '80s and early '90s, was traded to the St. Louis Cardinals. (Henderson has since returned to the team.)

Unfortunately, the young talent the Oakland organization was counting on to replace the older stars didn't materialize right away. For example, pitching prospect Todd Van Poppel was chosen with the number one pick in the 1990 draft by Oakland, but instead of developing into the starter to replace Dave Stewart, Van Poppel struggled with injuries and control and never reached his potential.

Tony La Russa, sensing that his time as the A's skipper had come to an end, left after the 1995 season to manage the St. Louis Cardinals. His 10-year stint as leader of the A's, where he compiled a 798–673 record, will long be remembered by Oakland fans as an era of great baseball.

Veteran catcher Terry Steinbach hit 35 home runs (2 grand slams) and drove in 100 runs.

A'S RESHUFFLE FOR THE FUTURE

The 1997 season (the 30th year of Athletics baseball in Oakland) had a promising beginning. First, fans of the long ball rejoiced at the return of Jose Canseco. Canseco, after stints in Texas and Boston, was reunited with his Bash Brother Mark McGwire for the first time since 1992. Hopes that the two players could vault the A's back into contention were running high.

But it was not to be. Canseco spent much of 1997 season on the injured reserve list and had a very disappointing season. McGwire, slated to become a free agent at season's end, was traded to the St. Louis Cardinals. The A's management feared that if they did not trade McGwire, they would lose him to free agency and receive nothing in return. Despite being traded by the only team he'd ever played for,

Versatile in the field, productive at the plate, A's star Jason Giambi.

A big piece of the A's future, shortstop Miguel Tejada.

Fans were watching Matt Stairs closely after his 27 homers, 73 RBIs, and .293 average the previous year.

McGwire made a run at Roger Maris's record of 61 homers in a year, falling just short with 58.

With Canseco injured and McGwire gone, the Oakland A's now pin their hopes on young, rising talent like 21-year-old infielder Miguel Tejeda from the Dominican Republic. Tejeda, drafted in 1993 at age 17 by the A's, had an excellent rookie season in 1997, impressing fans with his speed on the base paths and his defense at shortstop.

Other young players to watch include future star outfielder Ben Grieve and versatile slugger Jason Giambi. Grieve, known in the A's organization as the "Golden Child" because of his promise, hit .312 in 1997 after being called up from the minors. "Ben's the real deal," said A's manager Art Howe. "The kid can play, and we can't wait to see more of him."

Giambi, a second-round draft pick out of Long Beach State, can play several positions and shows vast potential at the plate. In 1997 Giambi hit a respectable .293 with 20 home runs and 81 RBIs.

Howe stated that he is giving players like Grieve, Giambi, and Tejeda a foot in the door. He explained, "We're looking to put together a nucleus for a championship club in the future, and they can show us they want to be a part of that [through hard play]."

But it is no easy road. Howe knows that with all the young talent will also come loads of mistakes, and victories may not come easily for a while. However, like founding manager Connie Mack in 1901, the current Oakland A's look to the future with optimism and a hope that their young players will become the stars of tomorrow.